SURVIVaL

of the

CHRISTMaS
SPIRIT

AIMEE HORTON

velvet morning
press

Published by Velvet Morning Press

This is a work of fiction. Names, characters, businesses, places, events and incidents are either the products of the author's imagination or used in a fictitious manner. Any resemblance to actual persons, living or dead, or actual events is purely coincidental.

ISBN-13: 978-0692467619
ISBN-10: 0692467610

Cover design by Ellen Meyer and Vicki Lesage

CHRISTMAS EVE

I stand in the dining room doorway and give a happy sigh of pride. Pulling my phone out of my pocket I snap a couple of pictures and upload them to Facebook, into my already bulging Christmas album. Now that the tables are all set for tomorrow's big dinner, I am finally starting to feel in control of everything. It looks better than I ever imagined; you can't even tell there are three different tables. What's more, unless you look really closely, you can't even tell that two of them are plastic outside furniture.

That's right, my dining room is filled with our normal dining table, two white plastic patio sets borrowed from my friend Jane and a last minute buy from eBay. If I'm honest, it didn't look great to begin with, but after much searching, the Internet came up trumps. Not only did I find a beautiful Christmas tablecloth that covered all three tables, but chair covers to match.

Leaning forward, I adjust the position of a tea-light holder, and faff a pile of sequins shaped like holly out a bit more.

Perfect.

I'm so excited. It's my first ever time hosting

Christmas, and I'm feeding eleven people. There's my mum and dad. My brother, Oscar, his wife, Laura, and their teenage daughter, Lexi. Then there's Henry's mum, Maria, and her third husband… Charles, I think. I can't keep up, to be honest. Finally there's us four. I've never cooked a Sunday roast for more than us lot let alone Christmas dinner, and somehow, eleven people are coming to witness it. But luckily it won't be a disaster; I've built a spreadsheet.

The kids have spent the day in front of the TV eating chocolates, and I've spent the day peeling veg and wrapping pigs in blankets. I've even had time to make an amazing chocolate log from scratch. All I need to do tomorrow is put things in the oven at the right times, and we're onto a winner. Even the presents are wrapped— usually we're still wrapping at nearly midnight. I can't believe how organised I am.

All that's left is for Henry to bring the turkey home tonight. Then we all snuggle up and read Christmas stories before putting the kids to bed, ready for Santa to come. While we're waiting, Henry and I are going to have wine and order in a pizza.

Not sure I can wait until tonight for something to eat though.

Suddenly, after all my hard work, I'm starving. I head into the lounge to grab a handful of Christmas chocolates, planning to crash out on the sofa with the kids for half an hour before I start cooking their tea.

Just as I'm unwrapping a green-foil-wrapped triangle of chocolate and deciding what topping to have on my pizza, my phone bings from inside my pocket.

Pulling it out, I try not to acknowledge how snug my jeans are, and instead look at the message on the screen. NO WAY—I can't believe it. I close my eyes for a few seconds.

Why does my mother always make life difficult for me?

Opening my eyes again, I glare at my phone and re-

read the message.

AUNT V UNCLE R HOUSE FLOODED. THEM MANDA JAMES AND TWINS COMING WITH US TO YOURS STOP. LOL MUM XXX

It used to take me ages to decipher my mum's text messages, but this one is as clear as day. At four p.m. on Christmas Eve, my mum has added six extra people—two of those toddlers—to the eleven I already have to feed. Oh, and she thinks LOL means *lots of love*, not *laugh out loud*—which would actually be more appropriate given the circumstances.

Two extra toddlers. That means three toddlers will be trashing my house while I'm cooking Christmas dinner.

Last time we had a toddler play date, all three had taken their nappies off and stuffed them down the toilet, nearly flooding the bathroom.

Dottie—focus. There are bigger problems than two additional toddlers.

There's not enough food.

Even though the turkey Henry is picking up is massive, there is nowhere near enough food for Uncle Rob's appetite. I've seen him devour a Sunday roast quicker than I can neck a gin and tonic.

I'm going to have to go shopping.

I can't imagine anything worse than the supermarkets on Christmas Eve but I have no other choice. After shoving a handful of kids' snacks into my handbag, I chivvy the children out the front door, through the pouring rain and into the car, tripping over the next door neighbour's cat.

Blooming thing is always getting under my feet.

The rain is rattling on my windscreen like Lego blocks on my old glass coffee table—the one that had to go after Mabel head-butted it and bled all over the white carpet that we'd managed to keep clean all the way through the Arthur toddler years. I peer through the windscreen wipers, and in a last ditch attempt to avoid the supermarket, I head for a cluster of local shops around the corner, and pull into the disabled parking space right outside the butchers. Leaving the kids in the car, I leg it inside. The bell jingles as I enter the nearly empty shop, and a woman in a striped apron looks up from behind the counter. The smell of meat hits me, and I feel bile rising in my throat.

"Turkey?" is all I can manage to pant, looking hopeful. The woman laughs and shakes her head, so I turn and race back outside, calling "Thank you anyway!" as I go. I stand outside for a second, breathing in the fresh air before clambering back into the car, my damp hair stuck to my face.

"There's nothing for it," I say as I buckle my seatbelt. "I have to go to the supermarket." I head to the nearest. It's small, but hopefully that will work to my advantage.

Judging by the amount of cars in the car park, I can tell it hasn't. After coaxing the children out of the car with the promise of sweets, I walk through the automatic door, take one look at the line at the tills snaking its way around the store, and then turn around, narrowly missing bumping into a woman with a heavy dose of coral lipstick.

"I wouldn't bother!" I say jokingly, smiling at her as I usher the children back outside, already promising they can have *two* packets of sweets at the next shop.

The woman grunts at me, and carries on into the shop, just as a man dressed in a royal blue polo-shirt with the shop logo on it walks out and deposits a sign reading "NO TURKEY OR PARSNIPS LEFT" onto the pavement next to the trollies.

I hope she was looking for turkey or parsnips the mardy moo.

"Come on, monkeys, let's go. We still need to find that turkey and get those sweets," I sing to my grumpy children as we run back across the car park.

Next stop ASDA.

I let out a low groan. I know it's going to be packed. It always is, but hopefully they'll be on top of stock control.

I don't even bother heading towards the parent and child spaces. I abandon my car in what feels like the furthest space, near the petrol station and car wash. With a child on each hip, I run as fast as I can towards the store. There don't seem to be any trolleys available, so dragging the children behind me, I head to the fridges. No turkeys. We head to the freezer.

Nothing.

There are, however, some really cute looking mini pigs in blankets, so I pick those up, along with a couple of packets of sweets and two bottles of prosecco that are on offer.

Practically a saving.

The children are getting impatient, and I don't blame them. The queues go nearly as far back as the store does, and the kids have eaten two packets of sweets each before we've even made it to the till.

Glancing at my watch, I realise it's already past their dinner time. "You guys are being soooo good," I say, squatting down to wrap my arms around them, wincing at the wee smell coming from Mabel's nappy. "So so good!"

They grunt, not bothered by compliments. "Are you guys hungry?" I ask, and just as I catch their attention, the line moves forward. "We have another shop to go to." I see them beginning to wilt, so I hurry on, desperate to win them over. "So how about we stop off at McDonald's and pick up dinner?" I sing-song. The kids respond by jumping up and down and clapping. Relieved, I ease myself up, my knees creaking as I do. Suddenly though, I find myself sprawled out on my front, my two bottles of prosecco rolling across the aisle.

What the actual…?

"The line's moved," says a voice behind me. Turning round, I look up to see the woman with the coral lipstick from the last shop. Her trolley sits exactly where I had been crouched moments before.

"I can see that," I say, smiling as politely as I can, picking myself up off the floor. I send Artie off to retrieve the bottles. Just then, the woman in front of me realises she's forgotten kitchen roll and leaves the queue, meaning I'm next. We shuffle forward again, and before I know it, we've paid and are already back in the car driving towards McDonald's, knowing full well where we have to go next. The Superstore.

Eurgh.

I go through the drive-thru, and place the Happy Meal boxes on the front seat next to me, knowing that saving them until we're in the superstore is the only way to avoid a meltdown. A meltdown I can hardly blame them for.

Driving through the rain, still recovering from the woman with the awful coral lipstick actually knocking me down with her trolley, I wonder just how busy the superstore is going to be.

I snap to as the imposing blue, red and white sign of the supermarket looms over the road in front of me. Taking a deep breath, I turn into the car park.

I've never seen it so busy. I crawl along looking for a space, and as I move into my third lap, I spot one. Suddenly, as I also spot a sports car headed my way, driven by somebody who looks suspiciously like the woman with coral lipstick, realisation dawns. If everyone is coming with my mum and dad, that means they're staying at my house too. In my two-bedroom house.

Bugger.

Zooming haphazardly between the white lines, narrowly missing the convertible as it tried to nab the space first, I park wonkily and turn off the engine. *HA.* Pulling out my phone, I text Jane.

Mother strikes again. Can I borrow your airbed and sleeping bags? I send, before quickly sending another: *Buying extra turkey, will be around after that.*

Shoving the phone in my pocket, I climb out of the car and grab a nearby abandoned trolley, fighting against the suddenly gale-force wind. Unplugging both kids, I lift them into the trolley, iPads, game consoles and Happy Meals included. They complain as the rain lands on their screens, but I make a mad dash across the car park, and we are inside before any of us gets too soaked. Trying not to notice the carnage of the last-minute shoppers packed into every square inch of the store, I can't help but spot my enemy following me in. I square my shoulders.

Right. Turkey.

Without stopping to browse the homeware section like I normally would—although do we need extra wine glasses?—I push the trolley determinedly towards the fridges at the back of the store. With the exception of a lone chicken, the shelves are empty. I turn, bashing a few buggies and an old man on a mobility scooter out of the way (don't look at me like that, I'm pretending not to notice what I did), and head to the frozen aisle.

As I approach, I see there is one turkey left. The coral lipstick lady is coming towards it from the opposite direction. I look at her. She's about my mother's age, but more spritely. Abandoning my trolley and the children in the middle of the aisle, I race over and grab at it. Our hands lock around the ice-cold bird at the same time. I look at her. She stares at me. I swear she's gritting her teeth. I open my mouth, about to explain my predicament, sure she'll understand.

However, she's on a mission. This woman, with her stupid lipstick, and her Marks and Spencer leather gloves.

This woman, who has already knocked me over once. She yanks the turkey so hard I have to let go. I fall back into the aisle, landing inside the trolley containing my two small children.

"Excuse me!" I call, clambering out in a rather un-lady-like fashion. "Excuse me, I really need that! I have four extra adults and two toddlers coming for dinner at the last minute… Their kitchen is flooded!" I totter after her as she marches down the aisle in the opposite direction. "Please!" I say as I rub my sore back and bruised calves. She doesn't even turn around, and I realise it's a dead loss.

No Christmas Spirit there then.

Standing in the middle of the frozen aisle, I try to decide what to do. Another supermarket is going to be just the same. There's only one thing for it: sundries. Slowly, I turn around and head back towards the fridges and the tiny chicken, grabbing boxes of powdered gravy and stuffing as I head to homewares. Only new wineglasses can save us now.

৩৵

Arriving home, I'm pleased to see Henry opening the front door as I park the car. Kissing my head, he opens the boot stuffed with sleeping bags and pillows from the ever-reliable Jane.

I plop the children directly in front of the television. The batteries on their electrical devices died at the till in the supermarket, but after a slight incident with a nearly stolen bag of brioche, the reminder that Santa is on extra-special watch while he's packing his sleigh was enough to keep them both quiet.

I'm unpacking the shopping when Henry brings in the last load. He drops it in the hall and circles his arms around my waist. I lean back and give him a kiss.

"I've done something… I hope you don't mind," he begins, standing in the door of our dining room. My stomach fills with panic. I hate it when he makes executive decisions.

"Okayyy?" I say, bracing myself, but not wanting to look worried.

Stepping aside, Henry waves his arm towards the dining room, which leads into the conservatory. The conservatory door is open, and the little table from Artie and Mabel's bedroom is now taking pride of place. It has a tablecloth and a variety of toddler-proofed table decorations, including electric tea-lights.

"How did you… ?" I begin, and notice the main table has been shuffled around as well. It looks amazing and accommodates everyone.

"Cut up a spare chair cover." Henry beams with pride.

I feel a wave of emotion and burst into tears. Sobbing, I run into my bewildered husband's arms and cry for what feels like forever.

"Sorry," I murmur into his shirt when I'm finally done. "I just thought we'd never fix it, and I have a stupid small chicken and hardly any food, so I didn't know what was going to happen, then you do this, which is lovely." Then I start crying all over again.

Henry smooths my hair and pushes me to arm's length, probably to save his shirt rather than to check if I'm OK.

"The turkey is huge, the chicken will be fine. Kids hardly eat anything, and as long as you have extra Yorkshire puddings, you'll be set." He smiles that smile he does to reassure me. "Now," he says, checking his watch. "Let's shove some food down the kids and get them into bed so we can open that new gin my boss gave me."

"No need to feed them, I got them McDonald's." I

beam, not only pleased at my own forward planning, but at the opportunity to inhale half of their Happy Meals.

Bolstered by the thought of the gin in the snazzy bottle, we get the children bathed and dressed in record time.

Well, when I say "we," I mean "Henry." I stay in the kitchen, making some last-minute alterations to the timetable for tomorrow.

There weren't that many alterations to make really, just add "put chicken in oven" half way down the timetable. But I really couldn't be arsed with the bath-time meltdown I knew would happen with an overtired Mabel and an over-excited Artie.

After tweaking the timetable, I rummage in the cupboard and pull out a bag of kettle chips. The strong salt and vinegar ups my energy level, and as I hear the water gurgle out of the bath, I take a deep breath and make my way slowly up the stairs in time to see Henry dressing both children in their matching Christmas pyjamas.

I grin. I always like them at the end of the day, when it's nearly time for them to go to sleep.

"Let's read on Mummy and Daddy's bed tonight!" I say, and together we all bundle under the quilt and read *The Night Before Christmas*. Mabel snuggles in close to me, sucking her thumb, her eyelids already drooping, while Artie on the other hand can barely sit still.

He's going to be trouble.

As we close the book, Henry scoops Mabel into his arms and takes her across the hall, leaving me with a hyper Arthur.

Sneaky sod.

"When is Santa coming?" he asks, bouncing up and down on my bed. "I'm going to see him, you know! Will he come in my room? Where's my stocking? If I put it under my window, he'll wake me up if he takes it out to fill it up." He fires off the questions in quick succession, making me regret leaving the bowl of chocolates in front of the CBeebies Pantomime.

I don't even begin to answer. Instead, I pick him up and cuddle him, carrying him into his bedroom, hoping that once he's in there, with an already fast-asleep Mabel, he will be quiet. "Shhh now, nah night, I love you." I lean forward, stroking his head.

"But I have tummy acheeee," he whines quietly into my hair.

"No you don't," Henry whispers over my shoulder, pulling the duvet up to Artie's neck before making a hasty exit.

Glaring at his departing back, I lean in to give my son one last kiss, and he wiggles his arms out and around my neck. "I can't get comfortable." His eyes are wide and innocent—a giveaway that he is totally lying about everything.

He's excited. I should give him a break.

Sighing, I sit on the edge of the bed and try not to think about my lovely gin and tonic going warm and Henry having full control of what pizza we're ordering.

"Santa only comes when you're asleep," I begin, stroking his hair. "So snuggle down, and think about the lovely songs from the Christmas films you've been watching."

"But I can't sleeeep."

"Yes you can. You haven't even tried."

"Noooo, I want to see him. Can I just come and kiss Daddy one more time?"

I lose patience. I'm hungry, tired and really want a drink.

"Artie, snuggle down and go to sleep. I don't want to tell Santa to take your presents off the sleigh." I play my trump card, even though I'm aware it's far too early.

"You wouldn't do that. He's already in the air. He's

already flying his sleigh. You told me so earlier."

I knew that bloody follow Santa app would stuff up my evening one way or another.

"Look Artie, this is your last chance," I say pulling out my phone. I've started it so can't stop now. "Go to sleep, or I'm going to text him."

I kiss him and turn to leave the room.

"If you message him while he's flying his sleigh, he might crash and die," my son says quietly from under his duvet. "Then you'll have killed Santa."

Give. Me. Strength.

"Then I'll call him," I say, although I know I shouldn't respond. I should just walk out of the room and down the stairs, but I can't help myself.

"Does his sleigh have hands-free, then? Because Daddy says if you use the phone while you're driving you could crash." I swear there's a meaningful pause before he says, "Don't worry though, Mummy. I haven't told him you text and speak to Auntie Jane while you're driving."

The little…

"Yes, it has hands-free," I say, forcing a smile. "Now go to sleep." I begin walking towards the door again and as I hear my son start speaking, the sound of the phone ringing downstairs rescues me.

"Mummy has to get the phone. GO. TO. SLEEP and DO NOT wake your sister," I say, louder than intended. Then I race down the stairs to answer the phone before it rings out. It's my brother, Oscar.

He speaks first, before I even have a chance to say a word. "Hello, how are you doing?" I realise I don't have the energy to rant.

"Thanks for rescuing me from bedtime hell," I begin, before answering his question. "As well as can be expected, I guess." I slouch down onto the hall floor and lean against the wall. Accepting a gin and tonic from

Henry, I wish once again we'd gone for a cordless phone instead of a retro-looking one. I look like a moody teenager on the phone to her boyfriend.

"I mean, what can I do?" I ask. Knowing he has no answer, I go on to list what food I have, and Oscar—who's a plumber—goes on to explain about the pipe that was under the flooring in Auntie V and Uncle Rob's kitchen, and how they'd been staying at my mum's all week.

I'm not really paying attention—too busy seething at my mother's short notice—when my mobile phone beeps from within my jeans pocket. Pulling it out, I swear without even meaning to.

"FOR FU—"

"What's the matter?" Oscar asks, stopping mid-flow in his explanation of stock cocks or something similar.

I re-read the text first to myself and then out loud to my brother.

DON'T FORGET MANDA AND JAMES ARE VEGGIES—TOLD THEM YOUD DO THEM NUTROST LOL MUM XX

"She told them I'd do them a nut roast?" I say in disbelief, taking a glug of my gin and wrinkling my nose in disgust. Either the new stuff is horrid or the tonic is different, because my usually favourite drink tastes vile.

Does my mother hate me?

"I can't actually believe she actually promised them an actual nut roast, and left it until seven-forty-five p.m. on actual Christmas bloody Eve when I haven't even had a chance to order my bloody pizza yet! Can you believe it?" I squawk down the phone at my brother. He doesn't say anything.

"Oscar? Are you listening to what our bloody mother has done?" I raise my voice, and Henry races in and points up at the stairs, reminding me we want the children to be asleep, not stay awake. I lower my voice and whisper, "Oscar?"

"Dots, you're in luck!" My brother is smiling, I can tell by his voice. "Lexi's boyfriend, you know the one who's in a blooming band of all things, he's a veggie. She says she can make something and bring it!"

I hear the voice of my sixteen-year-old niece in the background, and I want to hug her.

I'm just about to shower her with compliments when Oscar continues, "She also says she has some special gravy you can use." I sigh with relief. I hadn't even thought about different gravy, and tears of relief prickle in my eyes.

"Tell her she's amazing, and I love her, and I am just about to pop something extra into her Christmas present." I sniffle down the phone to my brother as we say our good-byes, confirming they'll be here for Buck's Fizz around eleven a.m.

Still feeling emotional, I spend a couple of minutes looking at the dining room to cheer myself up before seeing if Henry has ordered our dinner. All that talk of vegetarians has given me a hankering for a vegetable-topped pizza.

He's not in the lounge, and as I wander across the hall to the kitchen to see if he's there, I hear voices upstairs. Peering upwards I see my husband's long legs stretched across the landing opposite the bathroom door.

Artie is obviously having a delay-sleep toilet-visit.

Going to replace my gin with a glass of red wine, I spot Arthur's iPad on the counter and realise Henry is only halfway through the pizza order.

Oh my God, I'm starving!

I add a few more bits to the order and then, spotting an offer at the top of the site, I add an extra pizza and garlic bread to get an additional twenty percent off. Now we'll have enough for leftovers on Boxing Day as well. Turning to my overflowing wine rack, I choose a bottle of my favourite red, two wine glasses, and on a whim, I also grab the half-eaten bag of kettle chips from earlier.

I settle down on the squishy sofa in the lounge and put my feet up on the table, relieved once again that everything that can be done today is done. All that's left, once Artie is asleep, is to take the presents upstairs and fill the children's stockings.

I turn on the TV, switch the channel from some high-pitched, brightly coloured kids' animation to a rerun of *Home Alone 2*, then set to work on the rest of the crisps. Munching my way through a couple of handfuls, I am thrilled at how festive the room looks. The tree lights are twinkling, the logs are crackling in the fireplace, while the Christmas candles burn next to it. I can't help but get excited all over again about the thought of tomorrow, with everyone in here opening presents and enjoying themselves. I close my eyes for a minute and imagine if we had a piano how I could play Christmas carols and everyone could sing, like a really old-fashioned Christmas celebration.

Not that I play the piano, but still.

Just as I'm deciding whether I should go help Henry with Artie—who is trying every delay tactic in the book—I hear footsteps on the stairs. When Henry walks into the lounge, the doorbell rings.

"Perfect timing, honey!" I let him answer the door, not intending to move again until the stocking-filling and bedtime.

"How much did you order, Dots?"

I turn to look at my husband. Perhaps I did go a bit overboard. You can only see the top of his bushy hair over a pile of about eight, maybe nine, boxes.

"I've been a busy girl!" I exclaim, rubbing my tummy before clearing a space on the coffee table. Laying out a couple of old magazines to protect the wood, I continue over-justifying. "Plus, I thought leftovers for Boxing Day maybe?"

"My wife, classy as ever." He smiles, setting down the pile of boxes and ruffling my hair. I dive into the food, opening sauces and grabbing a bit from each box.

Settling back onto the sofa, I bite into my pizza, and as I begin to chew, my throat closes up.

Urgh.

I take a sip of wine and let the liquid soothe my throat and settle my churning stomach.

I'm still sweaty and weak, so after taking another sip, I grab a handful of crisps from the bag on the floor. The sharp flavour does its job and I begin to feel back to normal. Tentatively, I reach for a potato wedge, but can't quite face a chicken dipper.

It must be those cold fish fingers I'd snaffled from the children.

I look at the slice of pizza on my plate and the nearly full boxes in front of me.

"I'm full," I say, setting my plate on the floor.

"You shouldn't have wolfed down an entire bag of crisps." Henry rolled his eyes good-naturedly. I attempt to look shocked.

As he clears the food away, I head up to check on the children. I'm exhausted, so exhausted I can barely climb the stairs, but as I walk into their bedroom, a rush of energy runs through me. Even though it's only nine p.m., both of the children are fast asleep. I'm thrilled.

Grabbing their stockings, I whisper down the stairs to Henry, and together we sneak into our bedroom and stuff them. Tiptoeing back into their bedroom, we put the stockings at the end of their bed, not daring to kiss the children in fear of waking them up. Finally, I go back to my bedroom to put my pyjamas on.

Dressing gown wrapped around my still not-totally-settled-stomach, I spot next door's blooming cat curled up on my pillow. It must have snuck in when Henry answered the door.

Bloody thing, look at the mucky paw prints all over my duvet!

Scooping it up, I lecture it quietly as I trot down the stairs. I open the front door and gently evict it. Feeling slightly guilty, I remind myself of my now dirty bedding. I head back into the lounge to watch the Take That Christmas special and have a last glass of wine before Henry finishes the bottle.

CHRISTMAS DAY

I can't believe I'm the first person awake, especially after Mabel woke up at two a.m. and started unwrapping presents. Luckily, I heard her before it was too late and managed to re-wrap them. Hopefully it was too dark for her to see what she'd got.

Now, when she is nearly always up before six a.m., here I am, lying in bed at six-forty-five, and the house is silent. Well, except for Henry's snoring.

I lie there, straining my ears over the snorting next to me, for sounds of the children waking up. I'm excited to hear the squeals of their voices when they see Santa has visited. In fact, I'm so excited I feel sick.

Unable to keep still, Henry's snoring irritating me more and more, I go downstairs and pop the oven on. It will be good to get a head start and have it ready for the turkey to go in after breakfast. After flicking on the kettle, I check my colour-coded itinerary. Satisfied I'm on track—five minutes ahead actually—I grab a mug and open the fridge for the milk. I beam with pride at how well stocked it is.

I love a full fridge.

I make my tea and take a sip. It tastes gross. Gagging at the horrid taste, I spit what's left in my mouth right back into the mug. Eurgh, the milk must be off. Wrinkling my nose, I tip the liquid down the sink, and just as I'm about to wash the mug, something twitches in my brain.

Wait.

Slamming the mug on the counter, I spin around and fling the fridge open again. There's no turkey.

Bloody Stupid Idiotic Henry. I can't bloody rely on him for anything.

Racing up the stairs, taking them two at a time, I descend on the still-snoring lump in our bed, shaking his shoulder.

"HOW COULD YOU FORGET THE TURKEY?" I yell, not caring if I wake the children. "How could you be so idiotic to forget the bloody turkey?"

Rolling over, my husband looks at me through half-open eyes.

"What? Huh? What?" He croaks, brushing his slightly wild hair out of his eyes. It takes all my willpower not to pick up a pillow and beat him with it, before having a full blown Mabel-style tantrum on the bedroom floor.

"The. Turkey." I begin, through gritted teeth. "You were meant to pick up the turkey."

"I did!" Henry replies, eyes fully open now. And suddenly realisation dawns on him. "I left it in the boot of the car!" He looks relieved that he's back in control of the situation. "It was so cold last night, and I knew the fridge would be overflowing, so I left it in the boot."

"Oh," I say, feeling a bit guilty. "Thanks."

How was I supposed to know that?

I head quickly down the stairs, grabbing the keys; I'm now desperate to get the turkey inside and safe. I'm hit by the freezing cold morning as soon as I open the door, although I can't help but enjoy the winter sun on my face. *Perfect Christmas weather.*

Unlocking the car, I heave the huge bird out of the boot, somehow managing to close it again, before I stagger inside. Dumping the turkey on the kitchen counter, I turn to close the front door, but before I get there, a gust of wind catches it, and it slams shut on its own accord.

The noise wakes the children, and within seconds, shrieks of excitement echo through the house. I make my way upstairs to join in.

৯৯৫

"No, you can't have chocolate for breakfast," I say over my shoulder to a grumbling Artie, as I make my way to the kitchen. I see Henry sneak Artie and Mabel chocolate coins, and I smile to myself.

"How about a mince pie instead?" Mabel instantly claps her chubby, chocolaty hands together in delight, and Artie fist pumps the air in agreement.

Happily, I leave the room, humming my favourite Christmas song—Mariah Carey, if you're interested—as I go. My stomach is rumbling for a mince pie and a fresh cup of tea. Once I've had that, I can really get cracking. We're still ahead of time.

As I reach the kitchen, I stop and stare at the scene in front of me.

"NOOOOOOOOO!" I try to scream as I stand in the doorway. However, it just comes out as a choked whisper.

On the floor, in front of the fridge, is the turkey. Well, I say turkey, but what I should say is the *remains* of the turkey. On the windowsill, looking out over the garden is next door's cat, licking its lips.

I don't believe this.

"Henry!" I call, in a strangled voice. "HENRY!"

My husband lollops ... having to say anything, the smu... ball.

"What the actual...?" he begins, and without me turning to look at me. I assume he's trying to... I'm coping with the situation.

"We're screwed," I say, the panic setting in. "We are totally and utterly screwed." I stamp my feet on the spot and let out a frustrated growl. Launching across the room I practically yank the cat off the windowsill, then march to the front door with it held at arm's length. I'm furious with this animal.

The children have appeared behind me, wondering what the commotion is all about. "Was the cat bad?" Artie asks. "Maybe he should go on the naughty step," he suggests, ever the helpful one.

My anger subsides—slightly—and I plop the cat onto the ground. "AND STAY OUT!" I shout, slamming the door behind me. Brushing my hands off, I feel marginally better.

The feeling quickly fades as I see Henry picking shreds of raw meat off the floor. Artie and Mabel trail behind me. I grab a packet of mince pies from on top of the breadbin and pass it to Arthur.

"Kids, go into the lounge and watch TV and play with your new toys, will you?" I say, in a high-pitched sing-song voice. I was going for upbeat and in control but failed.

As they scarper across the hall, whispering and giggling at the opportunity to sneak more than one mince pie, I look at the kitchen, nearly clear of the evidence.

"What are we going to do?" I ask, shoulders slumped.

Henry hands me another cup of tea, but the smell of it turns my stomach. I set it on the counter. "The milk's off," I say, with a dramatic arm gesture. "Just ANOTHER thing to add to the list."

, s, shrugging before
" .e serious matter in hand.
"Tastes OK to me."
returning to the everyone," he says, putting his arm
Christmas. rest my head against him. "They could all
and bring something. I'm sure your mother has a
ozen joint in the freezer."

Urgh. My Mother.

"I can't think of anything worse than admitting to my mother that I've failed." But I know his suggestion is probably the only option.

"Do we have anything in the freezer?" he asks, and I shake my head. I'd cleaned out our tiny freezer only a week or so before in preparation for the big day.

Opening the fridge, Henry and I stare at its contents, which this morning looked bulging and full, and now look pathetically sparse. The three large pizza boxes containing the remnants of last night's meal are stuffed above the salad tray—mocking me and taking up valuable space, which could have been filled with extra pigs in blankets and roast potatoes.

"Pizza?" he suggests, half laughing.

"I'm calling Oscar." I stomp into the hall and pick up the phone, hoping my brother—or at least his daughter—will come up with another magical solution after last night's nut roast miracle.

◆◆◆

Unfortunately, this time my brother was unable to work miracles. In fact—once he's done laughing—it's clear the only solution was the one Henry had come up with.

I'm going to have to ask my mother for help.

So now we're not having turkey, but we have an assortment of various main courses, which I hope will go with the vegetables. Along with the nut roast, Laura and Oscar are bringing a cottage pie and chicken. Maria is bringing a joint of gammon, and my mother, along with a whole load of judgement is bringing some "nice sausages and a portion of sweet and sour chicken." It might not be the most conventional of Christmas dinners, but at least there should be enough for everyone.

We're going to be OK.

Now it's twenty minutes before everyone is due to arrive, and I'm showered, dressed, and attempting to tweak my well-thought-out spreadsheet, replacing things like "baste turkey" with "put cottage pie in the oven."

The house is unexpectedly calm, and I feel as in control as somebody can be when their—what I consider to be gourmet—Christmas dinner plans are turned upside down.

It's going to be fine.

Just as I'm getting ready to make another batch of Yorkshire pudding mix, the doorbell rings. Without even having to open the door, I know my mother has arrived. I don't know how, but I swear the doorbell sounds stressed and anxious. Just how she makes me feel.

Before I have a chance to prepare myself, the door is open, and our tiny hall is filled with people. My children squeal with excitement at the bags of presents in my dad's hands. I greet everyone as the twins belonging to Amanda and James burst into terrified squeals at the unexpected noise and unusual house.

"Why don't we all go into the lounge?" I suggest, starting to worry how everybody is going to fit into the small room.

"DARRLINGGG!" My mother sweeps in, handing me two rather-on-the-small-side, freezer bags. "What a catastrophe! I was so looking forward to turkey. We've even been having beef on Sundays to build up to the bird." She takes the glass of Buck's Fizz Henry has offered her and kisses me on each cheek. "I should have known when you mentioned you had a cat this would happen."

"Dirty horrible creatures," my dad says, turning to Henry and asking for a "man's drink" instead.

"It's not my cat," I say, for what feels like the hundredth time that day. "I told you on the phone. It's next-door's. It keeps sneaking inside."

"Well you shouldn't encourage it," my mum says.

Changing the subject, I look at the freezer bags.

"So erm... How many sausages do we have?" I ask my mother.

"Four. And a portion of the sweet and sour. Make sure the chicken is heated right through." I'm about to question how many people she thought we were feeding when she says, "That's one good thing at least. No turkey means at least she can't poison us all." She then makes her way into the lounge and repeats the exact same sentence to Val and Rob.

"I need a drink," I say, but before I can open the fridge, the doorbell rings again. As soon as we open it, the house is officially full. Henry's mum, Maria, and Charles are here, somewhere behind two massive bin liners decorated with tinsel. And behind them are Oscar, Laura and Lexi. The twins, who had just calmed down, start screaming all over again, and Mabel shouts at them to shut up.

A wave of nausea flows through me, and I take a deep breath before leaning in for kisses.

Henry's mother fusses with my hair and hands both children what appear to be life-sized replicas of puppies. "They are just the same as real doggies, except you have to plug them in to charge every night," she tells the children, as the one that looks like a Dalmatian does what looks suspiciously like a toy poo on the floor. A white poodle with a pink bow starts yapping loudly.

"I need a drink," I say again, and this time, as if by magic, my dutiful—and for once, very helpful—husband is by my side.

"Gin?" he asks, opening the fridge and reaching in for the tonic.

"You know what?" I say, my stomach lurching. "I actually fancy a Tango—is there one cold?"

Giving me a strange look, Henry rummages in the bottom of the fridge and pulls out a can. He's just opening it for me when Oscar comes in carrying foil dishes with cardboard lids, a large freezer bag and a frozen-solid pack of chicken thighs.

"Voilà!" he says, placing them on the kitchen counter. I grab the Tango from Henry as he leaves with two cans of beer for our guests. Gulping it back, I am relieved as the sugar hits my system.

That's better.

"No gin?" Oscar asks, opening the fridge, and reaching for a beer for himself.

"Nah, don't fancy it for some reason," I say, removing the lids from the foil containers and looking in despair as I realise that yet again, they're portions for two people, not nineteen.

"Not like you," my brother says, and then he laughs. "Last time you were off gin, you were pregnant with Artie."

Laughing, I punch him on the shoulder shaking my head.

"Daft sod. It's just stress," I say, although something starts to tick in the back of my head. But then my mind flicks back to the dinner ahead.

"Everyone likes Yorkshires, yeah? I don't need a special oil or anything for the vegetarians, do I?" I reach for the eggs and flour. "Go on through, I'll be there in a second when I've just mixed this batter—then we can exchange gifts."

It takes me two minutes to mix another jug of batter, then I stick the chicken in the microwave onto defrost.

Taking a last slurp of fizzy orange, I grab a champagne flute and head into the lounge in time to see Artie open a massive Spiderman remote control car from Oscar, and Mabel a Range Rover ride-on that needs charging up before she can ride it. Henry disappears for a few moments, returning with a couple of extension wires and multiple plug sockets.

I can't believe my two-year-old daughter has a Range Rover before me.

"We're going to have to buy a new house just so we have room for all these toys!" I say, and Henry rolls his eyes.

"Any excuse to bring up a house move!" he says, and I beam at him innocently. I've wanted to move for a while. It would be nice for the kids to have their own bedrooms now that they're getting older. And as much as I love our little terrace, the kitchen is quite old. Plus a laundry room so I don't have to hide the ironing on our bed when we have visitors would be amazing.

Just as I begin to dream about double garages and an en-suite, I hear my name behind me.

"Dottie!" I turn to see Val beaming at me, a gift bag in her hand. "I'm so sorry to land us all on you at the last minute." She hands me the bag. "Here you go. It's not much, but your dad assured me you'll love it!"

Opening it excitedly—I love a good present—I pull out a bottle of my favourite gin, complete with branded glass, and a little bottle of tonic. "Oh Val!" I say, "You shouldn't have!" I give her a hug, then head into the kitchen and set the bottle on the counter. Squatting down, I open the oven door and check on the chicken.

For such a small bird, it seems to be cooking slowly.

In fact, the oven doesn't feel that hot. Turning it up a bit, I jiffle some of the baking trays so I can slide the

Yorkshire puddings in. Then I set the time so I remember to come back when the oil is hot, before finally checking the chicken in the microwave. It's starting to defrost, but I put it on for another ten minutes just to make sure it's totally thawed.

God I'm hungry.

Reaching into the cupboard, I feel about until I find the nearly empty bag of kettle chips from last night. I stuff a handful of crumbs into my mouth, then another and another. God they taste good.

Just then, I hear a rattle of a plate. Uh oh. The chocolate log I'd so lovingly created had been placed on top of the microwave, probably when somebody was rummaging about in the fridge looking for drinks. Without even looking, I know what's happened. Sure enough, as I carefully pull the plate down, my beautiful chocolate log is a puddle of chocolate sauce and curdled Bailey's cream.

I look at it in despair, my eyes prickling with tears, as Henry races into the room with an empty bottle. He reaches for the kitchen roll.

"Don't panic," he says. "But my mum spilt some Buck's Fizz on the carpet, and your mum cleared it up with the red paper napkin…"

I don't want to look. I only had the carpet cleaned the other week, and already Mabel took her dirty nappy off on it, and Artie spilt a glass of Ribena over it. Taking a deep breath—come on Dottie, man up—I grab a dish cloth, and with a smile plastered on my face, head to the lounge.

The two women, obviously already the worse for wear after God-knows-how-many glasses of Buck's Fizz, are giggling like a pair of school girls on the sofa. And as my mother sees me, she sticks her foot out in a hurry, using it to cover the pink stain on the carpet.

"We can't take you two anywhere, can we?" I say,

forcing myself to laugh. I leave the room without even bothering to clean the stain on the carpet. I dump the remnants of the chocolate log in the bin and stand at the sink counting to ten. By the time I get to nine I feel a hand on my shoulder.

"Don't worry about it, love," says Henry soothingly. "I've Googled it and found a solution. We'll nip to the shops tomorrow. If everything's calm in here, why not join us for a second? Come and watch the kids trying to play TWISTER. It's hysterical."

Henry, ever the positive. But he's right. "I'll be there in a minute," I say. I put the defrosted chicken in the oven, and while I'm there, I shake the pigs in blankets and reset the timer. Then I put the cottage pie in the microwave to defrost and check the meatloaf, which is reheating in the slow-cooker. Finally, I grab my glass and head into the lounge where Artie is trying to do left arm green.

It's lovely, actually. The rug has been pulled over the stain, and my lounge is filled with laughter. People are lying on cushions on the floor or curled on the sofa, and the children are laughing hysterically as Lexi attempts to help Mabel do left foot yellow. Although I smell a strange odour coming from over by the twins.

My sister-in-law's glass is empty, so I grab a bottle of wine and top up her glass. As I set the bottle down, I see a trickle of yellow running down one of the little girls' legs.

Please no!

"Er… Amanda!" I squeak, indicating to her daughter. She jumps and scoops up the child, catching the yellow liquid in her hand. "Bathroom's upstairs," I say.

God, I can't wait for Mabel to be toilet-trained.

Cringing, I head back to the kitchen. This is the final run. The Yorkshire pudding, gammon, and cottage pie all need to be in at the same time, and soon the chicken will be out, and we can all sit down. Most of the vegetables are roasting with the chicken, the sprouts are on the hob, and the gravy is ready to go in the microwave.

Considering this morning's disaster, I think it's going to be OK.

It won't be perfect, but it will be fine.

Except—oh God no—I open the oven door and reach in for the tray of oil, and instead of the burning heat making my arms prickle, cold air does.

Flicking the heat up and down, I realise I can't hear the fan either.

Shit. Shit. Shit.

Walking as calmly as I can across the hall, I poke my head into the lounge. "Hen?" I say, keeping my voice surprisingly level even though I can feel the bile rising in my throat. "Can I borrow you for a sec?"

Henry stands up and makes his way into the kitchen, and as soon as we are out of earshot, I whisper, "The bloody oven is broken!"

"What?" We squat in front of the oven, wafting our hands in and out, turning it on and off at the wall. That's when we realise the microwave is silent, and the light on the slow cooker is off.

"Shit!" he exclaims.

Oscar pokes his head in. "Everything alright in here? We appear to be having a slight electrical fault in the lounge."

Great.

Henry and I head back to the lounge. Everyone seems oblivious to the fact that the lights are no longer on.

"What happened?" I ask my brother, who tells me he went to unplug Mabel's car and it hadn't charged, and nothing else had either.

We go from room to room, trying various plugs and sockets. They're all off on the ground floor.

It's just the fuse gone. Dinner will be delayed, but it's OK.

Henry and I check the fuse box in the downstairs loo using my phone as a torch. Sure enough, the fuse switch for the downstairs is off.

Phew.

Henry climbs onto the toilet, and balancing precariously, flicks the switch back on. I wait for the lights to turn on and the noises to begin, but nothing happens. I try the light switch. Nothing.

Shit.

"Try it again," I say, desperately, and Henry does. He flicks the switch up and down about five times before climbing down from the toilet.

"It's broken."

What are we going to do?

"What are we going to do?" Henry asks, echoing my thoughts. "I'm guessing dinner isn't cooked enough?"

"No, no Yorkshire puddings, none of the meat is cooked through and most other bits were due to go in the oven ten minutes ago," I say in despair. "The potatoes and carrots and stuffing are under a not-yet-cooked-chicken so I doubt they're safe."

"So what do we have?" Henry asks, and even he is beginning to look totally defeated.

I think for a moment. "I guess we could reheat the meatloaf, nut roast, and sprouts in the microwave upstairs on the landing?" I suggest, thinking that it didn't sound very appetising.

"Just meatloaf, nut roast and sprouts?" he asks, as we make our way into the kitchen. "With gravy?"

I open the fridge and pull out three boxes. "And pizza."

❧

Candles lit, everyone is gathered around the dining

table laughing. Laid out in front of us are plates filled with microwaved pizza, breaded chicken and wedges. There are also bowls of Brussels sprouts, nut roast, meatloaf and dishes with frozen garlic bread slices, which have been cooked in the toaster at the top of the landing.

I can hear the chatter in the dining room while everyone takes their places and corks being popped out of bottles of wine. As I'm carrying the last plate of breaded chicken out of the kitchen, I foolishly pop a piece in my mouth. All of a sudden I feel sick. Quickly, I force the plate into a passing Henry's hands and run upstairs to the bathroom. I empty the contents of my stomach down the toilet before leaning over the sink and washing my mouth out, panting.

When the feeling subsides, I sit on the closed toilet with my head in my hands. I really can't do with being poorly right now. It would ruin today. Because despite all the mishaps, it's been lovely having everyone here.

I lift my head, ready to brace myself and go back downstairs. As I do, I catch sight of a nappy bag in the bin, and my stomach lurches again. This time with fear instead of nausea. Oscar's passing remark about me going off gin flashes into my head, and I remember I couldn't eat chicken when I was pregnant with Mabel. I start to work things out on my fingers, and as I do, realisation slaps me in the face. I quickly lift the toilet seat and hurl again.

I'm pregnant.

Shit. Shit. Shit. I can't think about this now. Standing up, I shake myself and wash my face. I reapply make-up for good measure. Slowly I make my way downstairs and join my guests.

Henry is standing at the head of the table, holding a glass of champagne. As I sit next to him, he hands me my glass and makes a toast.

"To Dottie, who against all odds, the neighbour's cat,

the last-minute guests, the supermarket stalkers, and the blown-out fuse, has made us a wonderful dinner, and given us a fabulous Christmas I'm sure we'll never forget!"

That's for sure.

"To Dottie!" everyone says. "Cheers!"

Together we raise our glasses, and I set mine down without taking a sip.

"No champagne, Dots?" Rob asks, laughing.

"Oh, I'm just hankering after a slice of pizza—let's eat already!"

"No gin and no champagne!" Oscar exclaims. "That's not the Dottie we know and love. Come on girl, get it down you!" he says, topping up my glass.

Henry is still standing. He's been topping up people's glasses, but he's now looking at me.

"No booze, off chicken and eyes bigger than tummy…" he says, slowly. I cringe as I see realisation dawn. I shake my head, hoping he'll catch on that this isn't the time for this.

He doesn't.

"You're…?" he asks, sinking into his seat.

"I think I am…" I nod looking wearily at him, trying to pretend that there aren't seventeen pairs of eyes on us.

"But how?" Henry asks.

Oscar bursts out laughing. "I don't think we need that at the dinner table now do we Henry?" Then pushing his chair back, my brother takes the stand. "To Dottie and Henry—for making this a Christmas we'll never forget!"

"A Christmas we'll never forget!" Everyone laughs, their glasses held high. Except my mother of course, whose lips have formed a disapproving line.

And with that, my stomach flips again. This time, because I can't imagine how the hell I'm going to cope with three children when I can barely keep two alive. I take a swig of my champagne, spitting it out as I remember I can't drink any more.

It's going to be a long few months... pass the pop.

acknowledgements

Thank you to everybody who looked after the boys while I re-wrote Dottie's Christmas adventure.

Thanks to mum for reminding me how she nearly lost the turkey to the cat all those many years ago, to all my sanity checkers, and to Matt for providing me with lots of cups of tea and gin!

About the Author

Aimee is from Lincoln, England, where she enjoys drinking gin and spending time with her family (and she won't tell you which of those she prefers doing). As a child, one of her favourite parts of the summer holidays was to devour all the books in a little book shop in Devon. She continued reading at lightning speed right up until having children. She now reads with eyes propped open by match sticks.

Aimee hopes you enjoyed the book! If you did, she'd love it if you left a review at Amazon. For every review—even just a few sentences—Amazon sends Aimee a bottle of gin. OK, not really. But Amazon does help convince other people to buy Aimee's book, which is arguably even better. Depending on the brand of gin.

Want more? Get *Lush in Translation* for free! Simply join Aimee's mailing list: http://bit.ly/aimee-gin-news.

Check out the rest of the Survival Series, featuring Dottie Harris:

Survival of the Ginnest, a modern-day diary of a new mom.

Mothers Ruined, a riotous novel of Dottie's misadventures in suburbia.

Lush in Translation, a funny short story highlighting the differences between the British and Americans.

For more about Aimee, check out PassTheGin.co.uk. And you can always drop Aimee a line at mrs@aimee-horton.co.uk.

Read on for a sneak peek of *Mothers Ruined*...

Find out just how British Dottie is in...
Lush in Translation

Dottie Harris is as British as they come, which is exactly what endears her to us. But when her pregnant American cousin comes for a visit, Dottie is a frazzled disaster who can't seem to overcome the language barrier.

Lush in Translation is a funny look at parenting from both sides of the pond, and the surprising number of confusing language differences that entails.

Get it for free! Join Aimee's new release mailing list and she'll send you a free ecopy of *Lush in Translation*: http://bit.ly/aimee-gin-news.

MOTHERS RUINED

1.

am I THe ONLY ONe WHOSe PLaNS aLWaYS GO WrONG?

WHY THE HELL ISN'T HE PICKING UP HIS PHONE?

I'm speeding. Well as much as you can speed when you're stuck behind a tractor on what feels like a single-track road. There can't possibly be enough room to overtake, even though that posh-looking car has overtaken us both and is already just a speck in the distance.

I glance at the seat next to me, where a Tesco carrier bag stuffed with various snacks, fruit shoots and about five different electrical gadgets is resting, along with my hospital bag. By hospital bag, I mean random clothes rammed into the first handbag I could find that didn't have a layer of mini-cheddar crumbs crushed into the lining.

I didn't expect this baby for another three or four weeks. How the hell was I supposed to know it would bloody come early?

The nearly out-of-battery iPad is charging in the cigarette lighter, and my mobile is propped precariously on the dashboard in front of the petrol gauge. Stabbing at the screen again, I select Henry's number for the hundredth time and listen to it ring out. The kids in the back are irritating me even more by counting how many times it rings before going to answer machine. This time it's only three before the sound of Henry's "grown-up work voice" comes out of the tinny speakerphone and informs me he's away on business and will be back in the office next week.

He's bloody diverted my call! Three rings means he's seen my name and diverted it! Idiot.

Stopping the car on the grass verge, I grab my phone from the dashboard and Google Henry's Scotland office. He visits there every few months, yet I've never needed to call. I've always relied on his mobile phone to get in contact. However, this time it's serious.

"I need to talk to Henry Harris, please," I say to the Scottish voice on the other end of the phone. I attempt to sound calm, even though I can feel a niggling pain again in my lower back. The receptionist begins to inform me he's in a meeting right now, but with the cars racing past and the kids shouting, I can't hear her and lose patience.

"Look, can you give him an urgent message… no… I don't want you to get him to call me back; I need you to use these exact words: THE BABY IS COMING. GET YOUR BLOODY ARSE HOME NOW. Have you got that?"

It's times like this I wish I could slam my phone down instead of just pressing the screen angrily.

The pain subsides, and I try not to think about how cross Henry is going to be with me for speaking to her like that.

I suppose it was a bit rude.

But I'm having a bloody baby!

It's not enough that he pissed off on a jolly to drink whisky for nearly a week and left me to move house on my own with the two kids—oh no. Now he's going to miss the birth of his third bloody child, his second daughter. And yet again, I'm left to do everything myself. But I can't do it all. I mean, I can't even work out how to use the bloody newfangled baby monitor. It keeps screeching static at me or playing random music.

Starting the engine, I take a deep breath and carry on to the hospital. But all I can think about is: If I can't manage to operate the baby monitor, how can I look after three children on my own?

Arriving at the hospital, I reach into my bag for my wallet to buy a parking ticket, but I can't find it. Shit! I rummage about, but as I work my way through button-down nighties, big pants and feeding bras, the image of my lovely tan and pink leather wallet flashes in front of my eyes. It's next to the kettle.

How the hell did I forget my wallet? I NEVER forget my wallet; you never know when there's going to be a good shopping moment.

Sod it. I don't have time to worry about little things like parking tickets. Balancing a vile-smelling, nearly asleep Mabel on my hip, I grab Arthur's hand and make my way towards the entrance of the maternity wing. I'm nearly at the door when I hear a shout, and turning around, I see the traffic warden waving his hand, indicating my ticketless car.

This isn't fair. Why do they charge for parking anyway?

In a sudden burst of pain-free energy, still lugging my bag and the kids, I march back towards him. As I approach my car, I realise he's actually writing me a ticket. He's not even given me a chance!

"You going inside to get change for the machine?" he asks, not even looking at me. He holds the ticket in the air, in what I can only assume is an overly dramatic way of giving me one last chance to say I was going to get change. But of course, I don't give him that answer.

Instead, I squeeze between my car and the one parked next to it and snatch the ticket off him.

"I…" I begin through gritted teeth as another pain builds up, "am… in… bloody… labour…"

He opens his mouth, starting to say something as he attempts to take his ticket back, and that's when it hurts. Like proper hurts, and before I drop her, I thrust Mabel at him and grip onto the bonnet of the car, letting go of Arthur's hand and the parking ticket as I do. The traffic warden visibly recoils, and I'm not entirely sure whether it's because of the smell coming from Mabel's nappy or because the ticket flies into the air and is carried away by the breeze.

Where the hell is Henry? How the heck am I meant to deal with all this on my own?

"Let's get you inside, Miss." I hear the attendant's gruff voice, and holding onto the kids, he ushers me forwards. As we approach, we see a big sign on the automatic door reading "DOORS BROKEN. PLEASE USE REVOLVING DOOR" in bright red letters. The man moves through first, holding Arthur's hand and Mabel in his arms.

Through the glass, I see a look of panic forming on Mabel's face as she leaves me outside. Not wanting her to be scared at a time like this—I'm already terrified—I rush towards the door to follow them.

"Whose bright idea was it to put a revolving door in a maternity wing?" I mutter.

Taking a deep breath, I give the door a shove. It moves quicker than I thought, and one of the sections passes me by, then another. I jump into the next, managing to squeeze my big belly into the tiny compartment. I give another little push, hoping it will spin just as quickly, but my bag is blocking it.

Shuffling in farther, I drop my bag to the floor and try again. Nothing. My bump is too big; I can't get the right angle. Damn it! Mabel's calling my name. Her voice is on the edge, and she could start screaming any time now.

For crying out loud.

I turn sideways so that my bump is facing the middle, then take a side step. This time the door moves, and I manage to slowly sidestep round until a draft of air-conditioned air hits my red cheeks and the back of my neck. Collapsing into an undignified squat, I scoop up my bag before straightening up and turning around so I can make my way into the hospital.

Two young nurses and the car park attendant are trying their hardest not to laugh.

With as much dignity as I can muster, I wave at them, but in doing so, clout myself in the face. Instead of trying to save my dignity any further, I turn to the kids and point to some chairs next to a big television.

"Artie, here are some crisps for you and Mabel. Go and sit on those seats over there while Mummy talks to the nice midwife." I collapse into a nearby wheelchair, nearly knocking another pregnant woman over who is about to ease herself into it. She opens her mouth, ready to say something, but I silence her with a glare.

That's when I realise how serious the situation is, because while Henry will probably miss the birth of his child, the two small children already halfway through a bag of Pom-Bears might not.

I need a gin and tonic.

☙

"Something's not right."

The words ring in my ears, and my exhausted, aching body jumps to attention.

After I collapsed in the wheelchair, the kids were ushered off with a nurse, and I was wheeled in for an examination. I was only two centimeters dilated.

How can I be only two centimeters dilated—I thought I was at least eight!

It feels like I've been here for days. They started to make noises about sending me home, muttering things about "coming back in a few hours," but I couldn't stand it. I could feel my voice getting higher and higher as I told them how hard it had been to get here. How my waters had broken on the stairs after celebrating a successful poo in the toilet (Mabel, not me). How I'd assumed it was a huge wee, but then the pains kept coming all through the afternoon and the school run. That's when they changed their minds and whisked me off for another examination, promising me that the kids were perfectly happy and they would try to find out where Henry was.

That was hours ago, and now here I am, with those terrifying three words hanging in the air.

Something's not right.

"What's not right?" I ask, but it comes out as a whisper. Not that anybody is listening to me anyway. In fact, they're all whispering to each other. I turn to the midwife hovering next to me, but she avoids eye contact.

"What's not right?" I say again, louder, and I can hear the fear in my voice.

"Baby seems to be in a bit of an awkward position," she trills, patting my hand. "We're just fetching the consultant to come have a look." She is smiling and seems perfectly calm, but I can't get the words *something's not right* out of my head.

What am I going to do? How can I do this on my own?

That's when I remember Jane. My best friend Jane. She works on the children's ward. As soon as her name pops into my mind, I start to breathe properly again. She's at work today! Right at this very moment, she is somewhere in this hospital.

She'll know what to do.

In my excitement, I gabble at the midwife, who eventually understands what I'm trying to say, and they put out a page.

As we're waiting for Jane to appear, the doctor arrives. He's tall, dark and looks to be in his late fifties. He obviously recognises me, but I don't have a clue who he is.

"Dottie Harris!" he greets me. "I thought you were never going to have another baby as long as you lived!" His eyes are sparkling, and he has a smile on his face.

He must have been here when one of the kids was born.

"How is the young man?" he asks as he examines me. I start to tell him about Arthur and now Mabel, but he stands up and cuts me off. "This baby looks like it's going to be a monkey, breech, so we need to prepare for other options."

What does that mean? I can't cope with this.

Totally overwhelmed, I burst into tears. Just then, Jane runs into the room, closely followed by a midwife who informs me that while she's not been able to get through to Henry, his office confirmed he's on his way.

On his bloody way? If he hadn't gone to bloody Scotland he'd be here by now, telling me everything is going to be OK. Luckily, I have Jane.

Jane is already by my side, stroking my hair. After a few reassuring words, she turns to the doctor and asks what my options are.

Jane talks me through what the doctor said, and I look at her blankly. She realises I'm too far gone to hear anything in detail so pauses before saying, "They were going to try and turn the baby manually, but you're quite far along now, so you're more than likely going to have a C-section." Her blue eyes are full of concern, and she searches my face, waiting for my reaction.

The words hit me like a punch in the stomach. Either

that or it's another contraction. I irrationally blame Henry for all that has gone wrong.

Idiot husband. If we'd not bought that stupid house, I'd not had to start bloody decorating the bloody awful nursery and gone into labour. If it wasn't for him I wouldn't bloody be here now. Alone.

Just as I start ranting at Jane, the door flings open again, and a midwife shouts, "Sir... sir... please! Who are you?!" as Henry appears, closely followed by two security guards in hot pursuit. As soon as they see me half lying, half sitting on a hospital bed, my legs akimbo and my gown hitched up around my knees, they stop short. One turns a funny shade of green, and looking at his shoes, starts to whistle tunelessly.

Yeah, because he's the one in the awkward position... But wait. Henry is here?

"HENRY!" The tears pour down my face as he runs towards me and grabs my hand.

"I told you I'd be here!" He smiles down at me before winking at Jane who tactfully leaves the room, saying something about going to check on the kids.

I want to punch him, and I actually clench my fist, but another pain comes. Instead, I satisfy myself with squeezing his hand extra tight, making sure my engagement ring digs hard into him. To give him his dues, he doesn't even cry out in pain, although I kind of wish he would.

"How did you get here? It takes hours to drive from Scotland," I say when the pain passes. "I haven't been here that long, have I?" I look around, disorientated.

"I jumped on the first plane here." He smiles as he wipes my face and squeezes my snotty nose with a tissue. I feel a warm flush of pride grow on my cheeks. But wait a minute. This is Henry.

"You FLEW?" I'm unable to keep the disbelief from my voice. Henry would never pay for a direct flight; he won't even pay for the train unless it's on expenses.

Am I dreaming? Am I already in theatre? Have I died?

Laughing, he kisses my forehead and shrugs. "So, what's happened? Where are we now?"

"Well, I got stuck in the door on the way in after the stupid car park attendant tried to give me a ticket, and I thought the removal men had kidnapped Mabel, but I found her hiding in a cupboard, and the nursery is all painted. I painted it pink and was about to pull the carpet up, but then Mabel did a poo on the toilet, and that's when I think it all started. My waters broke on the stairs—don't worry, I cleared it up. But then she threw up on the slide in the school playground and slid through it—she stinks—and I forgot to put the washing in the dryer, and oh God. I was so rude to the girl at your office. I'm sorry. I was just so scared and… oh… shit that hurts." Another pain surges through me and snot bubbles come out of my nose. Great. I wipe my nose and cheek with his suit jacket.

"Shhh," he says, pushing my hair away from my face. Then turning to the midwife, he murmurs, "Is she delirious?"

Before she has a chance to answer, the consultant returns. After a quick examination, he announces the baby is in distress.

No, I don't want her to be in distress!

He fires out instructions to the room, which is suddenly full of people. Then he tells Henry and me that I have to go into surgery now, that it's not too late, and that I can have an epidural. Henry is trying to stay calm for me, but he's gone a bit pale and keeps clearing his throat. He clears it so often that I don't catch everything the consultant says—something about where Henry needs to go while I'm going through to theatre?

Everything is happening so fast, and I'm terrified. I'm being wheeled off, and Henry is left outside on his own.

"I love you," he shouts.

"Please don't put me to sleep! I'm not ready to die yet! I want Henry... HENRY!" I sob, and the midwife comes to calm me down.

"Dottie," she says, "listen to me. You aren't going to sleep. We're keeping you awake. Remember, you had an epidural with Mabel, didn't you?" She's gripping my hand and speaking firmly. "Henry can come in as soon as he's scrubbed up, but we have to get to work now. The baby is in distress, so the sooner he or she is out, the better. Do you understand?"

Nodding my head slightly, I say, "She. It's a girl. I want to name her Martha, but Henry doesn't think having two Ms is a good idea." I feel my breathing return to normal. "Maybe after going through this I can persuade him."

That makes the midwife laugh. She holds my hand as the anaesthetist explains what's going to happen.

By the time the needle has been inserted—it takes three attempts as I'm shaking so much—Henry is back by my side.

I have no idea what's going on. I stare at the ceiling, at the blue screen constructed by a sheet, trying to work out what's happening. Henry looks a bit green but keeps looking at me reassuringly, smiling and nodding as if everything is OK.

After what seems like ages, there is a bit of a kerfuffle, then, "Here we are. Wow, what a whopper!" But wait a minute. Now there's silence.

Why isn't she crying yet?

More silence, and I panic all over again as I watch/see the midwife wrap a pinky, purply, gross little body in a blanket.

"Is she OK? Is she breathing? Just bloody pinch her, OK?" There's a ripple of laughter, which is quickly covered up by a few coughs, then I hear it.

First a whimpering that gets louder and louder, turning into a full-blown angry cry as they whip her off to get weighed. I'm crying again, Henry too, and he's stroking my hair, and all of a sudden everything is perfect. Who cares about the horrible house, or a car that only has two back seats, or that Henry nearly missed the birth? He's here now; we're a wonderful family. Henry, Dottie, Arthur, Mabel and baby girl Martha.

"Well, he's a healthy weight, that's for sure," the midwife says. "Nine pounds, thirteen ounces. And what a head! There's no way you'd have turned this boy, and he obviously knew it!"

"She!" Henry and I both shout in unison, looking at the middle-aged woman who is carrying our still-crying daughter towards us. The baby's blanket is already stained with blood.

Seriously, how is she allowed to be holding babies if she can't even get the sex right?

"No, definitely not a she," she says, smiling, "I've been doing this a very long time, and I can tell the difference, you know." She winks as Henry and I glance at each other, confused. Then, lowering her arms so we can see the tiny scrunched-up red face, she says, "Congratulations! It's a beautiful bouncing baby boy."

Find out what happens next… pick up your copy of *Mothers Ruined* today!

Made in the USA
San Bernardino, CA
21 December 2015